PUFFIN BOOKS

STAR CRAZY

Valerie Solís was born in Edinburgh in 1952. She lived for many years in Barcelona teaching English until she discovered her love of writing and painting. She has published books for children in Spanish and Catalan as well as in English. Valerie now lives in Cardiff and works as a holistic therapist and writer and illustrator of children's books.

Some other books by Valerie Solís

PINK FOR POLAR BEAR

Star Crazy

Written and illustrated by
Valerie Solís

PUFFIN BOOKS

PUFFIN BOOKS

Published by the Penguin Group
Penguin Books Ltd, 80 Strand, London WC2R 0RL, England
Penguin Putnam Inc., 375 Hudson Street, New York, New York 10014, USA
Penguin Books Australia Ltd, 250 Camberwell Road, Camberwell, Victoria 3124, Australia
Penguin Books Canada Ltd, 10 Alcorn Avenue, Toronto, Ontario, Canada M4V 3B2
Penguin Books India (P) Ltd, 11 Community Centre, Panchsheel Park,
New Delhi – 110 017, India
Penguin Books (NZ) Ltd, Cnr Rosedale and Airborne Roads, Albany, Auckland, New Zealand
Penguin Books (South Africa) (Pty) Ltd, 24 Sturdee Avenue, Rosebank 2196, South Africa

Penguin Books Ltd, Registered Offices: 80 Strand, London WC2R 0RL, England

www.penguin.com

First published 2000
Published in this edition 2002
3 5 7 9 10 8 6 4 2

Printed in Hong Kong by Midas Printing Ltd

British Library Cataloguing in Publication Data
A CIP catalogue record for this book is available from the British Library

ISBN 0–141–31534–2

Go-go the little penguin lived right at the bottom of the world. He loved his frozen home. But sometimes he wished he wasn't a penguin at all!

1

The problem was that Go-go
hated swimming. He couldn't even
dive. What he liked was the sky.
Go-go knew the names of all the
different stars in the sky and which
ones were brightest.

"I wish I could fly up to see the stars," he sighed to his mother one night.

"Penguins aren't meant to fly through the air. We fly through the water," laughed his mother. "Why don't you dream about the sea? The sea has its own magic."

But Go-go only wanted to think about the stars. "I wonder what makes them twinkle," he thought, as he drifted off to sleep.

One night, the stars put on an
extra-special light show. It was the
best Go-go had ever seen. Suddenly a
huge ball of light with a long glowing
tail appeared. It was a shooting star!

4

The bright star crossed the sky
and vanished from sight.

That night, Go-go couldn't stop
thinking about the star. Where had
it gone?

He decided he would try to find it.

Go-go woke up early the next morning. He was very excited and told his mother his plan.

"Please be careful, my little Go-go," she said, waving goodbye.

Go-go looked for the star all morning, but it was nowhere to be found. He sat down on an iceberg to think.

All of a sudden, there was a loud
WHOOSH sound. A spout of water
flew into the air! What could it be?

Go-go saw a little whale.

"Hello, I'm Blue," said the whale.

"What's your name?"

"I'm Go-go," said Go-go. Then he told Blue all about the fantastic light show and how the star had raced across the sky and disappeared.

"And now I'm looking for the star!" explained Go-go.

"I wish I could see the star too. Can I help you look for it? Perhaps it fell in the sea. We could dive down to the seabed and look there," suggested Blue.

"I'd like to, but I can't dive," admitted Go-go.

"A penguin who can't dive!" exlaimed Blue. "Come on, I'll show you how."

Blue dived down into the water.
After a moment Go-go followed
him. It was easy!

When they reached the seabed,
Go-go couldn't believe his eyes.

The fish sparkled just like stars.
Jellyfish flew through the water like
comets in the night sky.

But Blue nudged Go-go gently.
"Come on, we've got to find the star."

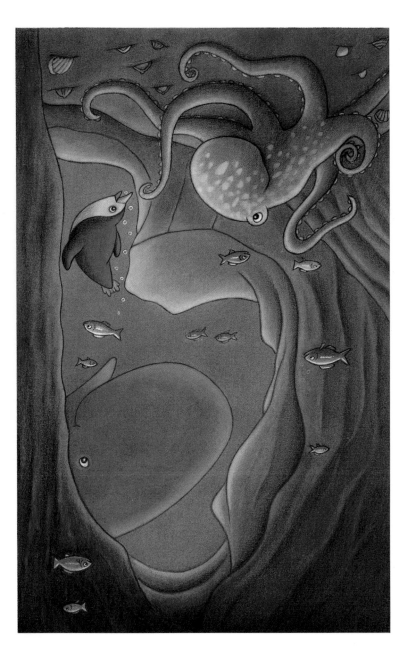

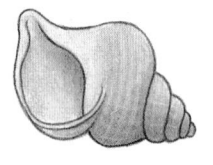

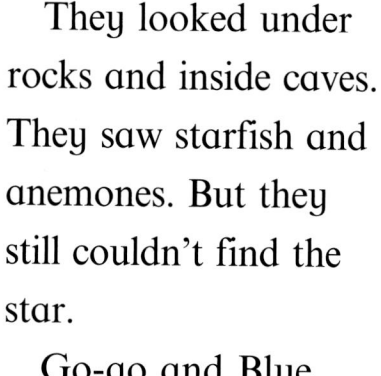

They looked under
rocks and inside caves.
They saw starfish and
anemones. But they
still couldn't find the
star.

Go-go and Blue
dived deeper and
deeper. As he
looked around,
Go-go thought the
sea was the most
magical thing he had
ever seen.

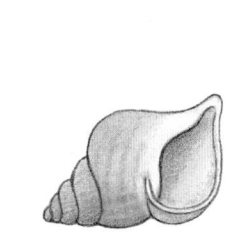

Suddenly, Go-go noticed a trail of
glitter.

"Look, Blue!" he exclaimed. "Perhaps
the glitter comes from the star."

They followed the bright trail along
the seabed until they reached a forest

of kelp. Inside, it was too dark to see.

"Oh dear, we've lost the trail," said Go-go. "What shall we do, Blue?"

Just then a small flashlight fish appeared.

The flashlight fish went inside the kelp forest and lit the way.

Go-go and Blue smiled at each other and followed the fish.

At last they found the star, resting on the bottom of the sea, amid the ruin of an old shipwreck. It was caught in a sail.

But the star wasn't sparkly at all.
All its glitter had fallen off.

"Why doesn't it sparkle?" asked
Go-go sadly.

Blue said, "It needs to be in the
sky to sparkle. We'll have to think
of a way to take it back up."

"I know, Blue!" Go-go exclaimed.

"We can use the sail to pick up the star and all the glitter. If you could do a big spout, I could take the star up to the sky in the sail."

"I can do a giant spout. I'm the best spouter in whale school," said Blue proudly.

Go-go put the star into the middle of the sail. Then he swept the glitter back into the sail with his wings. Blue helped him with his tail.

Together, Go-go and Blue carried the sail and the star up to the surface.

Go-go clambered into the sail. Blue got ready to spout.

WHOOOSH! Up flew Go-go and the star. Soon they were high in the sky.

The star began to sparkle! Go-go
knew it was time to put it back. He
threw the star out of the sail into the
sky. It stayed there, twinkling with
the other stars. Go-go held on tight
to the sail, which floated down like
a parachute.

Go-go landed gently on Blue's back. Together they looked up at the sky. There, up among all the stars, was a star that shone more brightly than the others.

"Look! There's our star," said Go-go, pointing to the brightest one.

"It's the most beautiful and sparkly one in the sky," Blue replied.

Blue took Go-go back to the shore and they said goodbye.

"What a wonderful time we've had," said Go-go. "Thank you."

Go-go told his mother all about his adventure.

"At last I've been up to the sky. It is very special, but the sea is just as beautiful. And now I love to dive!" said Go-go.

Go-go still dreams about the stars.
But he dreams about starfish too.